To my husband, you said I could do it and I did – thanks to your unwavering faith and confidence.

To my daughters:
Sadie, the pickiest eater I've ever known, and Ellie who will try just about any new food for the small fee of $1.00.

To Jorgie, our friend at the local donut shop who made sure Sadie always had her chocolate glazed donut holes.

To Dr. Matthew Hajduk and Dr. Dasha Solomon who have been advocates for Sadie and relished in her progress alongside us since the very beginning.

To my neurodivergent friends, trying new things can be very scary, but if Sadie Sloth tried spaghetti and my Sadie tried something other than a donut, then I know you can too.

© 2022 Lauren Walczak

All rights reserved. No part of this book may be reproduced or transmitted in any form or by any means, electronic or mechanical, including photocopying, recording, or by any information storage and retrieval system, without written permission from the author.

ISBN 979-8-218-09874-2 (hardcover)
ISBN 979-8-9878849-1-1 (paperback)
ISBN 979-8-9878849-0-4 (ebook)

SADIE SLOTH
AND HER SPAGHETTI

By Lauren Walczak

illustrated by
Daniel Wlodarski

Sadie Sloth is one of the cutest, funniest, happiest little sloths you could ever meet! She loves accessorizing — wearing bows in her hair, bracelets on her arms, and a big smile on her face.

Sadie loves to twirl and swirl and spin… but today she doesn't feel like twirling and swirling and spinning. Today the little sloth has a big problem.

Sadie loves string cheese.

Sadie loves string cheese so much that she won't eat anything else. But Sadie's mommy tells her it's not healthy if you only eat string cheese.

"Eating different kinds of foods will help you grow big and strong!"

Mommy Sloth wants Sadie to try something else.

This is a big problem.

"Look at all these different yummy foods!" says Mommy Sloth. Sadie looks at all the different foods, but she is not impressed.

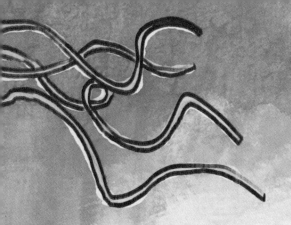

"String cheese is still my favorite. When I peel the cheese and make the strings, they are wiggly and wobbly and swirly! It's so wonderful and scrumptious," Sadie says. "And I can twirl and swirl and spin string cheese!"

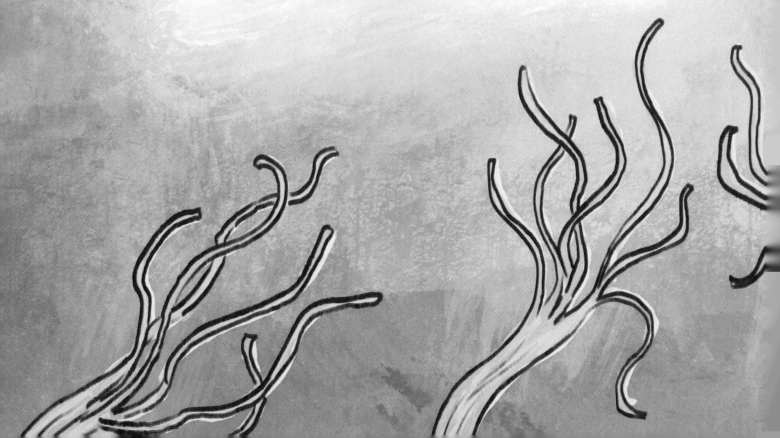

It's almost lunchtime and Ellie Elephant has come to play. Sadie asks Ellie if she has ever tried any new foods.

"I really want to grow big and strong, but what if new food tastes yucky?" Sadie asks.

"I was once scared of trying new foods too. I used to only eat éclairs. They are so delicious!" Ellie grins. "But my daddy told me I would only grow big and strong if I start to eat different kinds of foods."

Sadie can't believe what she's hearing. "That's what my mommy says! What new foods did you eat?"

"The first new food I tried was toast. My daddy said it would taste a lot like an éclair, a little bit crunchy and a little bit chewy, and he was right!" says Ellie.

"Wow!" Sadie is amazed. "That sounds so easy! Do you think I can be brave and try something new?"

"I know you can! Let's ask your mommy!"

The girls tell Mommy Sloth that Sadie wants to try a new food.

"Are there any foods that taste like string cheese?" asks Sadie.

"Spaghetti is a yummy food that is a little soft and squishy like string cheese." Mommy Sloth shows Sadie and Ellie.

"Can I hold it?" asks Sadie.

Mommy gives some spaghetti to Sadie and Ellie. They put it between their fingers, squeeze it, pull it, and look at it very closely.

"It does look just like string cheese!" says Ellie, surprised. "Let's try it!"

Mommy Sloth gives each of the girls a plate of spaghetti and a fork. "This is how we eat spaghetti." Mommy takes her fork, sticks it in the spaghetti and starts to twirl it.

"That looks fancy and fun!" says Sadie.

Sadie and Ellie grab their forks and start to twirl their spaghetti. This new trick makes Sadie feel super fancy. They giggle and have lots of fun twirling their new food.

"Now it's time to take a bite," says Mommy.
The girls look at each other. They are a little nervous.
"I've got an idea," says Ellie, "let's count to three and
try it at the same time."

Sadie nods. The girls take a deep breath and start to count,

Mommy Sloth is very happy. "Eating new foods doesn't have to be scary, it can be fun! Next time we can try to accessorize your spaghetti by adding a meatball!"

"Wow, Mommy, that sounds so fancy and fun!" says Sadie, jumping up. She twirls and swirls and spins out of the room. The little sloth no longer has a big problem!

"You can be brave and try a new food like I did!"

Author Lauren Walczak is a mother of two daughters, one who has Autism Spectrum Disorder. Familiar with the challenges that parents face in the kitchen, she spent years engaging in different therapies and interventions and her girls will now eat a wide variety of food – she hopes to encourage others to not give up. Thankfully, her two dogs Teddy and Louie are sure to eat anything the girls don't want! When Lauren isn't busy writing or working in the kitchen, she enjoys all things coffee and is a fairly decent tap dancer. She has a degree in Supply Chain Management and loves the color green.

Daniel Wlodarski is a creator of children's book illustrations, book covers and is an animation artist. He lives in a tree house with his wife, two sons, and a daughter. When he is not drawing, he is floating on a tire swing, dreaming about what clouds taste like, and holding his breath for a time. Visit Daniel's website, danielwlodarski.com.

Made in the USA
Middletown, DE
03 December 2023

44580799R00015